School Diaries

MRIDUL NANDA

BlueRose ONE.com
Stories Matter

First Published in December 2022

ISBN: 978-93-5704-307-6

BLUEROSE PUBLISHERS

www.BlueRoseONE.com

info@bluerosepublishers.com

+91 8882 898 898

Cover Design:

Aveek

Typographic Design:

Rohit

Distributed by: BlueRose, Amazon, Flipkart

Dedicated to

This book is dedicated to all my friends and those who knew me through school. Thanks to all teachers who supported me to become who I am today. I appreciate all the experiences and thankful for it which school provided me.

Cheers to all!!

Acknowledgements

I would like to thank my family for supporting me for making this book and having it in your hands.

Thanks to my mom who supported this idea when I was going to discard the file, thanks to my father being different from others and supporting me and how can I forget my sister thanks Vanini for making it a true and wonderful story being the first copy read by my family I am sure it will be a successful book and even if it fails to do so I am grateful for making it true for having a book with my name on it.

Foreword

First things first, this book is not centrally aligned on my idea of how school was this is the experience of almost every school going child. The vocabulary is not that amusing when compared to other books and there's a reason because the clear idea comes from simple words which I have chosen.

It contains all the experiences that I believe are crucial to know for those who are going to school and for those who have already gone to school it is just recap of what you did when you were in school.

I believe after reading it you are going to remember your gang and call them about what we did in school and yes, don't talk here and there just come to the point that I want to spend time with you all.

Let's not delay and do the inauguration of the chapters to be taken in account.

See you at the end.

School diaries

One third part of life is spent on education and 90 percent of that is in school and yet no one has been able to describe what we have done in school. Now if ou are already passed out and working in a high end job or bussiness this book will make to remember the glimpse of the precious moment of your school life. If you are a student then you will get to know about what will happen in your later school education. So hang tight and enjoy the moments gonna happen or already happened in your life.

Contents

Admission

Every time from the start when one enters the life form first two years go with happiness which none of us remember unless you are ***Sheldon***, but most of us don't. As soon as your age gets suited for the school, your parent's worst headache is not how our child will stay away from us but which school to choose. Now that they are not that good with Technology trust like searching on Google "The best school for my child." but even if they do this, they will not send you there. Parents will go all around the best schools father and mothers will start asking their neighbors for reviews of their child's school. They will fill out the form, and that's just the beginning, isn't it? The real headache starts now as if the child is not enough for the school, and the parents are also getting admission to the school according to the school. But you can't argue with them unless you are a millionaire and arrange a new school where you can study alone, which wasn't in my case. My parents filled out many forms, and wherever I used to go in the interview, I had made acceptable blunders as a child; come on, what do you expect of 2 years child to sit correctly and ask for everything before doing anything? In my first interview, the school's principal asked me which color shoes I was wearing, and I put my shoes on the table and then told the color. I even took the toffee, which was a drill that if I throw the wrapper in the dustbin, but guess what? I played a six and put the wrapper in the pocket. **"CLEANLINESS ACCEPTED"**.

School tantrum

I mean, who is such an idol soul on the earth who was living such a lavish lifestyle? They didn't even have to clean their poop and were being served everything they ever desired; instead, I do not wish for it, but if possible, I could ask for anything. Ta-da, it will be in their hands due to the cuteness and love. But all this eventually ends when you guessed it: school time. Who doesn't like to go to school? If I talk about myself, I wasn't such a superior soul, unlike you, so I hated to go to school. Ya, school life is a hell of a lot exciting, but I didn't know this from the very beginning, you know, and some things are just left to experience yourself in life like school experience.

I remember the school van used to come to pick me up. I was in my Kinder-garden, and the friend I made there was tremendous. All the teachers in the kindergarten were annoyed with me. Now they didn't know they gave admission to their problems. I was very highly energetic. I know the words I use are not correct, but in the true sense, they are so; I used to do all the work and study before the teacher taught it thanks to my mom till my 12 grade, I didn't ever felt the need to spend my half of life into tuitions and wasting my life along with money, yet not getting numbers now back to this chapter. I used to get into every fun activity possible with my friends throwing water onto someone, and sometimes things took the worst part also, which was when the teachers called the parents at home, which I think isn't needed, but you can't teach teachers, can you?

My parents used to give me a lesson. For some days, I used to put my job aside and work on some peaceful, fun activities, which were hiding belongings of everyone doing something and becoming a monk like I didn't know anything, and eventually, blame came on someone who didn't.

Now, who can forget the tantrums we used to play to not go to school? I remember that I used to search the ways to avoid school on the internet. The ideas that I got phew more than surprising; some told me that start was eating extensively, while others said to start coughing extensively and show tired signs. Also, one of them was not to sleep; some even suggested jumping from the first floor; all of them were useless to me, which made me get ***100 percent attendance award*** which I kept getting until my 10 class. All this continued until I learned I had to leave kindergarten for further studies.

Part 2 new life

Now I'm not going to repeat my admission process. Still, I got into an international school, the number one school in Faridabad not at that time but now it is.

The life which I got to know was now at a whole new level as you know the best the school more the tantrums of it.

The teachers were not at all angry at me. At the same time, they were happy that someone was there in the class who was able to everything running to the classes to do their work in; both the teacher and my motives were satisfied her work was done, and I was able to spend some time roaming I the school.

School teaches us a ton of different things, but which are other than studies; the first time I got to know there are bad words was in school, and when we didn't know what they meant but sounded the best to speak, which got into the daily habit of us. Communicating it to the teachers was the worst part of it the teachers took us to the coordinator, and at that time coordinator was like the Principal, which gave me a hell of guilt even cried in front of the teacher to let me go, but when the things take a turn you either get saved or get into more danger same was with my friend when he did say it to the teacher the parents were called and we all group of friends was named as the witness of his adorable activity. When the coordinator told the parents what happened, the parents of my friend asked if it was taught in school. Still, when the argument got heated, he was finally asked to tell from where he learned the word, which was funny cause the explanation he gave was hilarious; he said that "When the teacher was sitting in the staff room the other day, he came there but didn't go inside because she was talking to someone on her phone and used this bad word" when the coordinator heard this the teacher was the one got explanation punishment rather than my friend.

Ptm

The best part of the school parents-teacher meeting its general meaning is to point out the limitation in the interaction of children in school and at home, but school has changed its significance in a whole new sense. We used to get the invitation for the parent teaching meeting in the almanac, and all our friends used to discuss this topic for the current week what we had done so bad that we would get scolded. Further to make the child feel horrible, our teacher used to put the black star against the name on the attendance register which was placed at the entrance of the class being notorious of all I get the most of them which were put me in the great danger while bringing parents in the PTM. When my mom and dad used to come to the PTM, they already knew what was going to happen and even knew the dialogue; the teacher would say, "your child is very energetic he does his work and disturb the others study wise he is awesome but he does not let me teach in the class." Which got me grounded every week when this horrible PTM happens. This was the reason i tried 21 different sports till now and finally got to know where i belong.

The best part when the PTM is over is you generally get to see other parents of your friends or enemies who know your parents very well and discuss what the teacher told in the PTM. Come on, please change this either send the result online or tell these parents to mind their own business; what do u want from the other child focus on what is happening in your own life.

Lets move ahead!!

Sibling and relatives in one school

The whole new thing starts when your sibling or your relative friend joins your school. In my case, both of these happened. My younger sister joined the same school, but i didn't get into as much trouble with her as it was with my so-called cousins. You can easily bribe your sibling, do her work treat her with her favorite ice cream chocolate, or gift her a toy. But what will you do about those who are waiting for your mistakes to tell your Parents? Many of us must have faced this you get called into the coordinator's office, or you indulge in any of the fun activities, which mainly means doing some naughty things. Your parents will get to know you before you do because of your relatives.

The best thing to resolve this for those who are still facing this is to make a group of friends and make your relative a part of it in this way; he can't even say your name at home, and neither can you.

You get a whole new level of image when your sibling gets into school; the teacher presumes what the younger sibling will be if the older one is this. That's why i had to make an outstanding image in front of all the teachers to ease my sister from this image trouble.It was not like I didn't did anything if it would have been the case then the chapters of the book would have been segmented into 2 chapters not many like now. But all that wasn't needed because she already was a bright child, and all my efforts were for nothing; if I had known this before, then i would have done 5 6 more events.Siblings are better than cousins I should highlight this point and if you only have cousins then that's something you have to deal with either change your school or make your cousin change the school You know how.

Let's get on to next chapter of my school life.

Lunchbox

The best part of the school is the lunchbox. Thanks to my mom, she always used to cook something new as she was the chef and all my friends finished it before i could even see it. Whenever my friends got the chance to put a hand on my bag my lunchbox used to be completed when I opened it with excitement at lunchtime and when I used to confront them always heard that your lunch in way too good from us hearing it I could not even say anything, on the one hand, they were giving compliments. Still, on the other hand, they were misusing it.

We will describe some more about it, but from all this, i would like to share an event of a lunchbox that our school used to do.

All the students would get a notice of lunchbox exchange party, which at that time and now also excited most of us; we would get the menu for the items that we are actually no parents are required to send to the school for their ward.

When this usually started in a class, all were made to sit in a circular arrangement, and everyone had the lunchbox in hand. Now comes the exchange part. The teacher would take all the lunchbox and distribute it in a random way, but no, you won't get your lunchbox again; what i got was chapati and ladyfinger, which raised my eyebrows like, what in the world is this? It was not on the menu we were supposed to bring; I hate to eat it even when it is made at home i try to avoid it at my best. I tried to manipulate the other student sitting beside me, and you know, told him that it has sweets which i don't like cause my teeth will be harmed, and so on he gave me another lunchbox in exchange of the ladyfinger one. I escaped with the lunchbox and when I opened it it was more from a ladyfinger "the bottle gourd" i came back to him and said i don't want your lunch and luckily he didn't piss me and handed over the lunchbox in exchange for his. Now when I thought I should try again with other friend got to know he brought empty lunchbox because he thought that today all that menu that we were provided with to bring with us, he thought that it was going to be served to us today in the school so he had only brought his lunchbox but me being a gentle soul gave him my entire lunchbox and got dishes from every lunchbox instead of this.

School also brings you out of your comfort zone that i realized on that day when my food habit changed, but after going home, i don't know how my mom knew that I didn't get any favorite food in school, so she made me lasagne which I ate with my all senses and enjoyed every bite of it.

Now you might be hungry so let's meet in the next chapter; until then, have excellent food.

And abide by the menu next time.

Seating arrangements

The best part of the class is the seating arrangement, generally done when the session starts or when the teacher gets annoyed with all the students. We all used to fight for sitting next to our best friend, and there is always one child for which all of us fight to sit with he might be a sports person you best friend or a student of your class teacher, and for making a good impression or for getting questions for the following paper you all have to do this.

Then there comes those who always want to sit, at last, known as the backbencher, and also some want to sit in the front seats.

There has been a new definition of the students, which is in regard to the seating arrangement. The teacher guesses the idea of the student knowledge the one who sits in the front seat is always considered bright, and if there is any nuisance in the class, it is always put onto the ones sitting at the back. At the same time, this was an absolutely wrong interpretation of the students.

In my group, all of them were the ones who used to do playful activities while we were also the ones to top in the exams. So we were successful in proving the teachers wrong.

Sometimes, for punishment, the teacher also gives you the penalty of sitting with girls if you are in coet school which is generally everywhere and the teacher doesn't know that from inside you always wanted to sit with her we make nasty faces, but from inside we are so happy. That was with my friends itself. But it doesn't lasts long because the teacher herself forgets that whom had I made him or her sit with whom and if you have unity in class which was lacking in mine then you are on advantage side.

Sometimes the teacher even remembers your faces by your sitting arrangement, and she will say that there is that student who sits here. Then everyone will start shouting names of all the students one by one then also the teacher won't be able to get the name of the student until she or he sees him or her with eyes.

Exams

They were more of a challenge than a test showing the child's capabilities in different fields. We used to get informed about the date of the exams around two weeks before. Just after knowing the exam dates, there is just a new environment that starts Prevailing in the classroom. Everyone listens to the teacher carefully with all their ears to the teacher just so as to know the essential questions for the exam. Those who didn't even study started asking doubts, but you can imagine what their doubts can be like; mam, if 2x2 is 4, then how 1x4 is also four just like this, how stupid can you get to know these doubts write all these on the next page.

All used to come to school just for study by the topper student, there is always one in the class who is a topper or who does analysis every second of his life and we who never used to talk with him/her but now we fight with each other that who will sit next to her for clearing the doubts or getting a summary of the chapter. Giving him or her a promise to give treat in the canteen.

Exams are more of a pressure, yes; I agree with the fact that pressure is an essential thing in life to grow to beat all the circumstances in one's life. Still, students are forced by parents due to an environment like this where marks are everything; they are like you have to get more than him; otherwise, on the result day, what will I say to her that my child got 60 percent? He will show off her student marks by getting 99 percent; the student also gets demoralized that if he is doing all this hard work to get better in his studies or for that ***SHARMA JI*** ka ladka or ladki, they all are identical, just have to be Sharma.

Back to exams, the strategy that was to be made by all for getting the best marks without studying for the whole year and dreaming of getting full marks within two weeks of the exams. Who doesn't do that? Even when you are fully prepared, you to have to do everything again.

Thanks to the online platform that helped all, or i should say, make impossible dreams given reality. Still, only until the result of the exam was in our hands, we all used to search on Google for how to get full marks. Many ridiculous videos said that cheating makes good relationships with the teachers and many worse ideas possible, but the best one was to group study.

That was the part for which you all must have been waiting eagerly, but before starting with it, how many of you have actually done this or remember the one who did it?

In our group, we were 8 in total and all planned to do group study now the plan was made in the school but as soon as we reached home something was like sorted in the school got a hell lot of hurdles in our was like where to study and who will come how many more.

After a whole lot of discussion and fruitful ideas, when everyone's parents did not wish to bring students home, it was finally my left to make this plan successful which i was able to complete. Now the place was finalized. But now, we had to divide the study portion to be done from everyone's side so that we could crack the exam by an ace.

When everyone reached my home after all the similar events that took place in the god of war, that's when the actual group study began. We all placed our books aside and started playing play station in my room; at that time, it was something everyone wanted, and luckily, my birthday was that month, so it gave me no doubt in choosing my birthday gift. In a group study, everything happened, but the study was not the part of it for which everything was arranged when everyone got their home; I knew that even if i did not study from today itself, I could then also get at least 90 percent no doubt, that the study was challenging. Still, my mom, from starting of the session, was dragging me much ahead of the syllabus taking place in school while others at that time spent time in there hobbies which is actually more amazing. Still, i don't miss that because it was not extinct from my life, but it was controlled that if 4 hours study then 1 hour you will get from your own time.

All that just explained one thing if you are planning for group study forget it and do at least one chapter; that would be better, of course, unless you have a topper group.

Sports block

Now every part of school life is a bit more exciting than the other one, ***that's the secret, but this part is way*** more exciting than the other parts. Everyone wished for more sports blocks from the substitution table where all the substitutions are written. Usually, teachers bribe the students with this and even give punishment in the form of this, so it gets way more exciting. At the time when the teacher's syllabus lags more, or she thinks that these students won't let me complete my syllabus on time, she either takes away the sports block or utilizes it to complete the syllabus. Still, she even says she will give her a block if you let her finish her syllabus. Still, that day never comes; if she meets her syllabus, she will give it to some other teacher to complete their syllabus, but that's a dead investment because all the motivation for which all the students are coming to school, the teacher takes away that itself, so the time we had invested in taking sports clothes from our wardrobe to look good during sports stay inside the bag itself.

But now let's suppose you have reached for once, surprisingly in the sports block but that's not it, now everyone has to make a line and obey what PE teacher says, or you won't get on time which usually takes 10 minutes unless you are the child of the owner of the school. The teacher would ask you what you want to play but then will give his advice which will be his order that if he wants to say that you have to play basketball, he would say let's play football as basketball has no air. Still, he doesn't know what will happen next; some students will bring the basketball, which is as complete as your stomach, but we obey his say partially, as we play football but with basketball that's where our both objectives got fulfilled.

Now let's see how we used to play in our mode, whether playing football with a basketball or playing volleyball with a football; one thing was similar we always played with each other. Now when I see all those with whom I spent so much time are busy in their own life, I know it's good to look ahead in life, but forgetting your childhood friends is not acceptable. Hence, if you are still in school, make sure you promise your friends that they will remain your friend; if you take from at least 20, you might get 1 out of it.

Now let's get on to another chapter.

Monitor the savior of the teachers

Who must not know the story by just reading the word ***MONITOR*** of your childhood or your current time. The monitor is considered the savior of the teachers in many ways; when the teacher gets out of the class, you will see she keeps the monitor to keep looking at the children so that when she enters the course again, she will not have to waste at least 15 minutes in settling down the children that's when you will see the importance of the monitor.

The one who becomes the monitor has a different level of status among the students of the class; he might give you the threat of writing your name on the blackboard even if you are not doing anything but a close enemy of his. I got into this kind of trouble once the time had come, when the monitor had to be changed, which is usually one month. Then you can get retirement without any perks, but instead of helping out others, you will have to give money which is something i can't give comments on it; otherwise, the teacher reading this book will know all your tactics and strategy going to come in the future.

Let's get on with the monitor; when i got changed from the position of the monitor, the one who was appointed as the monitor was none other than my enemy at that time which was because he took away my stationary box and hid it, which took me two days to find out. When he was made monitor, that's the day when i took a fight in the class; for close to around ten times, he, without any reason, just *started poking me, and when it was high time, i smashed a punch in his face* and just kept on going after knowing the whole situation he was removed from his position and demoted to the clerk as in the one who gives books from class to class rather than the teacher. So monitoring word has associated many stories with me.

The monitor can also be used to bribe you like the teacher might say that if you let me teach in the class, i will make you the monitor, but after the end of the period, they will be like, you did something in the course which she can't remember but has compensated this with today. Unless you have someone you completely trust, ensure you don't give away your behavior or, most importantly, don't waste your precious time.

Worst subject

This topic needs no introduction. If talking till class 10, we can quickly agree that this award should definitely be given to MATHS. Come on, who can disagree with the one who says that I got the best marks in it which is me also will know the efforts it took to achieve that level, while the score was pretty much identical with less hard work in other subjects but we all know that being a practical subject it requires more efforts. This one has many stories from my side; for the first time, I scored less than 25 in any subject out of 30 in maths, and I had a streak of 21.5 from 5 of my unit tests no matter how hard my efforts were the paper kept on going from bad to worse. I even talked to the teacher regarding this, and I was unable to perform the sole reason she thought it was a lack of practice. I didn't know how much exercise I needed; my mom gave me 50 questions every day about maths, which also gave me a significant boost in my grades. I received 95 percent in maths in boards, which I am thankful to my parents, especially my mom, who were going to 5 to 6 hours of tuition. I then also received those grades without any help from anyone; just trusting myself was the most important thing at that time.

There is something ubiquitous in all the Maths teachers that they are very, I should say, self-obsessed; they think that if they told something that is important, the student would know everything and who knows might write a book. When asked about some questions that they find difficult, the teachers would say that let's keep this for tomorrow and that they never come or they will already come prepared the next day from Google.

This is it for maths and your worst subject, which might be based on this sort of experience. I believe that its not maths that is difficult but the way of teaching it is more of a tought job for us. The teacher would proudly say that ask a doubt a thousand times but as soon as it reaches to 5 the teacher stops explaining it and make fun of you that's what my friend faced due to which he neither understood maths in class nor in tuition which made him take medical stream in class 11 but when he got to know it was not his cup of tea he took commerce without maths. So just change the way you are learning.

Tution with school teacher

Many of us, must have gone to the tuitions of the teachers of the school for the reason that you will get the answers of the question appear coming in the exams or if you are intelligent to get more marks than what you are getting but, once you take that decision you must think thrice at least because from my experience once you have joined the tuition of the school teacher if u decide to leave that tuition in future you will regret that even if she or he not teach up to the mark or even teaching what you know already and think that this can be done at home also but then why am i wasting my time here some of us must have gone there because all of our friends do that is one of the most obvious reason for joining the tuition and i myself agree even i have not gone to any education but what from i heard from my friends this is somewhat very much enjoyable moment of life when the friend is there in tuition and when he is even in your class there is some sort of solid bonding that begins to form and in turn he might be your best friend till your life .

Getting back to why you should think thrice, let's say you have taken the courage to leave the tuition, but now let me briefly tell you what will happen the teacher in school will target you. She might make you stand to answer any question which might be out of your league. Still, to embarrass you, she might take this step so be careful even after that you may face high level to checking done in your exam sheet you might not get good marks in you internals you will meet the rumors made by her among the teachers but some teachers are completely different they will do everything in there limit to get a good score from you and generally the teachers should be like this only as there is a constant band of motivation which causes tension in your brain and you get motivated to score well.

Senior and junior

This one is one of my favorite chapters and, in reality, the best part. It is always that you are junior to some and senior to more, but that doesn't mean it is some sort of punishment. More senior means more you can learn from them, or in other words, they can make you understand.

Back to what I say, senior and junior lote {are made from love and hate}. Having your best friends from seniors is itself a part of pride in yourself. You might get more attention in the school classroom among all the batchmates you might even get away from the worst fights that can happen with you in the school just because you are friends with seniors. You might have your sibling as your senior, for which I did was that I used to drop her in the classroom with her bag on me. At the same time, her class was just a floor below my classroom but to increase my sister's power; I did this; you must have done some sort of this act only but in a different way if you have really gone to school.

I was having a hell of popularity in my school, or you can say what I wished I say. I was popular among teachers, but among students, everyone knew who I was. I kept my circle small just because I focused on the main things and made my senior's perfect friend. Many of them were in the sports which I played. I have made another chapter on it, so don't you worry about which whole explanation is given there. So I got into one big trouble in my entire school life: I had to face my principal, which even led to a call to my parents. That was a tough day for me; what happened was I fought with one of my classmates, and he called his friends from senior class; now, most of them he called were already knowing me, so most of them didn't bother to even show up after learning the matter the fight was for the word that he spoke which I couldn't tolerate I slammed him badly with the chair on his face. I punched him in his face, which led to bleeding, and that was very much intense for me also, being from a very polite nature, some take you for granted and underestimate your capabilities. Still, when it goes over your head, you have to control it, which I could not. When my parents got to know, they knew I never fought with anyone, and when told in front of the teachers, they also considered my act was right in my place, but it was more than it should be, so they gave me a name of punishment they said to go halftime from the sch00l. I couldn't think of any better day to remind me of my anger, but it was only one time in my whole life, and currently, also, that motivates me to leave all the worst things that I can get into.

So if you really want your seniors to be to get benefit to ask them the tips of studying and that too from who actually does study it should be like that you ask from someone how to study who says that I have not studied yet for my final and you are asking me. So make your senior your role model.

Now coming to junior, there is another level of hype that being senior, you can dominate all those who are junior to you, but that's a wrong concept you have seen or been taught the junior come to the rescue when no one can they can help you to whether it is your help in homework or it is your election time they can be of your great use in life as friends and as a helping hand.

Now let's move on to a new chapter.

Elections

Elections are an integral part of our country, and it has not been changed, but just some more modifications have been made not in the country elections. still, there have been some more elections that have taken place or come into existence in the recent while; the school elections are one of the best ways to get away from all the classes you don't like and get to know all the students in the school giving speeches posting your banner designing it making new connections making your rivals your best friends just like what happens in politics treating all the teachers like they are the favourite one. Giving the bribe in the name of chocolates and canteen party yes the elections contestants have to spend quite a lot of money just for the sake of cleaning and taking care of the school property I don't understand what power comes with elections I was myself like this contesting them winning it and when I got to know this is nothing but some additional security for the school in the name of power you are provided with one badge for which everyone spent nights for designing the poster and making strategies for winning the elections using the rumours of the opposing candidate for own benefit or making them. There are not all the disadvantages but some advantages too you get to know your juniors and making good chapter. You built a lot of communication skills making the right decisions at the right. The best part is when you win the elections, and you have to take responsibility for the school: nothing will happen to the school, and you will be a true in completing your responsibility as a saviour of the school. for this also you have to give a party to the students, and you can not be removed from this duty even if you want in real elections people fight for winning, and once you have taken part in these Elections, you will never give any advice in contesting them again to anyone.

School bus

It is like going on a water park ride which you never want to stop, but you also wish that it should reach faster to your destination. In my experience, those who have never gone on the school bus have missed a bit best part of the school. Our school had many buses, and finding the right was a very big task for me when we were in the primary grade. then the teacher accompanied us, and it was her duty to make the students settle in their respective buses. If this would not be done, then half of the children might have stayed in the school only. Coming back it was the mission impossible task. if you had been given a proper mark that what route number it is, it would have been easier for us, but our school suggested that maths classes should be given at every moment of time, so they decided to make new riddles like 44 plus 22 divided by 2 and so on to make students maths practice but little did they knew that it was gonna create a mess out of the students. It caused so much confusion like riddles changed every day and were put up on the buses, so you could not predict which bus was yours. I always used to wait a while before going to the bus area because that caused me to save my efforts as I did not use to focus on the riddles but focused on the bus students because they were not gonna change, but riddle does. Once the way was made to the bus sometimes, it happened that the bus was over occupied the teachers and the students had to stand up to make space for sitting of everyone those seats which were made for two accompanied 3 and 3 ones 5. This was indeed one of an enjoyable experience. We also used to jump at the time of speed breakers, and in case you think how many times that was infinite, being in India, you can expect everything out of the road, but one thing you can't expect is subtle roads with no breaker. Whenever there was a chips packet opened, many new friends came to enjoy it and have a share in it but as soon as it got finished, **hum aapke hain kaun**.

Also, ragging is one of the most common abuses in the school bus. The seniors used to bully all the small ones, and I saw it with my own eyes, but ones they tried to do the same with me, I reported it to my principal, which resulted in the suspension of that child. One should always know how to fight back. I strongly urge those who are currently reading this should always stand against bullying. now coming back to the topic, as I was saying, the school bus has its own life fighting with the bus driver for going from this way so that to reach home first or last. You can make many friends just by bus you get to know many more from your own locality which you hadn't seen, that's just surprising for me as when I got on my bus I realised that the majority of them were those whom i have never seen in my colony. It is really exciting to make ew friends and specially the ones in your colony. One gets to know a lot about the circle in which we live and helps in socializing.

Let's get onto the next chapter if you have completed your bus ride...

Medical room

The best place in school to escape from everything and complete your sleep which we had sacrificed to get to school .Getting away from the revision test or from the boring block that which substitute teacher has come up with. The real hype was that how to reach there because you know teachers are not themselves fool you have to do something extraordinary to get there showing the symptoms of headache would not alone work you have to do something special like acting as you are not well run out of the classroom and show as if you are gonna vomit out and many more such tactics you know better. This is one of the best moments to get away from everything. If you consider me, I have never bunked any class ever, but now i don't regret it because that was compensated with the enjoyable moments spent in the classroom during that boring block with all my awesome friends. There are many moments that never go out of your sight, and every time you remember them, you tend to laugh and remember them over and over again. but all this comes to an end when you finish the school all those friends you promised to stay with get away from you slowly, slowly but now is not the time for that; many more chapters are yet to come. This sad part one will be for the last.

Continuing this one, of course, in the medical room, there is one more advantage if you ever feel to go home early, you can act like you are not well, and boom, it happens the call goes to your parents, and you are at your home. I have tried this more than 10 times, and the medical teacher knew every time i went there, she was like, wanna go home? i would say yes, and she calls my father or mother, and they take me home but sometimes when the call gets done doesn't mean your acting should stop ,don't stop the acting unless you are escorted to the car; otherwise, the teacher gets to know, and the plan fails.

Our school also used to organize some tests like BMI, eye check-ups, and all that sort. It was usually done in the medical room itself. The day used to be random, and it used to be really exciting to go during and study block for these medical check-ups. There used to be a long line because two classes at least were called together, so the teacher used to say stand in one line, don't talk. like how is that possible when you keep two friends together the talk can not stop at that time, and you expect us to be quiet when there are 70 children together anyway; at one time 4 students used to enter in the medical room and let me take the example like at the time of BMI 4 students were called according to to roll numbers and then what happened in our case was first all 4 were measured in terms of height weight and strength the one who was saying that my weight won't be more than 90 got his weight to be 130 kg and i was a sportsman so my weight was around 70 and i was fit. That's when you have a high end than your friend, and he gets all scared. tat, don't tell it outside.So yes, these were some of my experiences in the medical room.

Your sports competition

Being in a school where all sports are accessible is nothing more than a wish come true mine was granted thanks to my parents, who spent a huge part of their money on my school, which helped me a lot in life. you must have tried many sports in your lifetime but when I was 13 I had played over 27 sports now that might not be great number for you but for me that's a lot you can get that from that number only that I never stayed in any sports for more than 3 to 4 months and finally the time came when i found the sport I was capable and made for shooting not that film one but real rifle shooting with all the equipment and in movies which we see the shooter never misses a shot that hard training is in reality which I have been doing for the past 6 years now I can easily shoot at least an eye of the coin from 10 meter easily I didn't knew that our school had shooting when I got to know that trials are going to get open for all the students I hurriedly took the form and choose my sport as shooting I also thought that this must be the photography one but got to know about that after I reached the shooting range there is whole lot of gear you have to wear for shooting and rifle that's just too hot to handle it's like you become a gangster and everyone is afraid of you yourself feel proud calling yourself as shooter. So coming back to the competitions there are competitions like interschool and different kinds of championships that are arranged or students from our school take part in it is itself an excitement among all the school students to watch the match if it is football then go to the school playground doesn't matter which class is going on leave it and the teacher themselves get excited to see it. The whole class goes to bunk; actually, it is worth missing a class seeing all that energy and that realistic cheering for the school on both sides. It's just awesome; it's just like the real match of football and cricket.

When the match is won by our school it's just so exciting among all the part of the school, and all the spectators would run up to the field and pick up the players, it's just an unexplainable feeling. I am sure that you must have gone through that feeling or are going to be exposed to it if you are in the school otherwise you can fell it from the words itself. Now we have always studied that sport man or women let's not be racial, have always been taught to respect their team members we must have heard if you play any sports in most of them teamwork is most important. Coaches scream and make the athletes work towards an awesome performance and make them capable of being down to earth, but that's just in the field or not there also. The sport athletes have two different attitudes and images in front of the class on the ground in the class. They must be like that we are the one,

Powerful and respectable in the school and no one other is like me, I am sure that there must be someone whom you must have got in mind reading it, they want everyone to serve them and treat them with respect I am also saying that's with only few of them so if you are not one of them don't take it in your heart or just learn these things not to be done by you this attitude word I never even heard it and once I got to know it from the school itself it plays an important role but I don't know how students manage to get into too much of mysterious world like in which they themselves get trapped making enemies come on who are you mafia or a gang boss the school or for enjoying and learning just got into emotions mind me if i wrote too much so coming back doesn't matter what you play where you come from just treat everyone equally which I learnt from the school life those who do not have friends be the first one to hold there hands as friends treat them the way just like you like to be treated from the world and that's the truth karma comes back and if its good then it will be more than what you did. Just keep faith and never get an attitude if possible.

Staff room and magical stories

We all know the place where our test papers are made and dreamt to be burned down into ashes which never happens , and neither do I hope for it, the place where all the teachers enjoy the gossip and microwave their food for an auspicious day come to life which is actually every day. the place where the students are discussed about each and every act they do in the class doesn't matter during which period you did it, but the class teacher gets to know all about it from other teachers where students are strictly prohibited for their work, but when it comes to pick up books of whole class from one classroom to staff room, all rules are meant to be broken. It's an awesome place just like the students have their hideout in the school the teachers have there own you might get lucky to get the revision test of tomorrow and might even get to know the marks of your classmates before the announcement which is itself an excitement news which I got to know a lot and exposed all those who said that **yaar maine toh kuch nhi kiya** they are the actual ones who get the maximum marks and top the class and those who say the paper was quite easy and I have done all the questions they don't get the answers right and the general comment of the teacher is that the answers you have written are right, but they are of different question. I mean, what is all the point of studying if you don't know where it is to be used? that's actually a very big problem in our education system that everything is about marks doesn't matter how good are you at other skills but if you are not getting good marks you can not get skilled according to school. What is the point of rote learning and vomiting all at the exams and also knowing that it won't be used or hardly used in life? One should focus on making the students learn about the skills that will help one get true success in life, making students learn about advanced skills, and making trips to the real office environment so that they can learn how the real work is to be done. Getting over this point, I would conclude by saying that smart work is more important than hard work.

Now, coming to the magical stories continuation, we all must have thought about many incidents that seem impossible but have arranged all the plans for it even knowing it won't happen like the attack on the school. What will i do? How I will become the saviour of all whom I will save first and all that endless stories. One of them in my experience must be how I will escape from the school when the time comes, and I know all have tried to execute it, but when it comes to trying it, we all know what happens next; our mind on their own only stops us, and we also think that what will happen if we attend the school for one more day and please keep it that way only it won't be fruitful for you to go missing out from the school I have seen many experience in our school that someone gets out of the school and then there parents and school authorities, concluding that's all for the magical stories.

Gate pass

Our school had a very strict rule about the gate pass which is used for the entry and exit of the school students and who goes on its own transport. For saying, it must seem to be an easy task and yes it is if it is on normal school days on the contradiction no day in school is normal yet on the more normal school days it is quite easy to get it and even it is easy on the days when your parents themselves come to school to get you.

The main challenge starts when you have to get out of school. Then it doesn't matter if you have written letter by parents, class teacher and coordinator you will have to wait for an hour for such a short process you have to run towards every teacher to get a sign doesn't matter if she knows you or not you have to get a sign and teachers don't give there sign easily as if I am gonna take a part of there property you will have to explain everything where are you going why are you going have your parents allowed it does principal know about it and all other questions this was not like this before,

There are mainly three sign required one of class teacher one of the principal and one of the receptionist of the school every sign was easy to get but the efforts were more than just a sign I remember two of my classmates once got caught they planned to get out of the school and to see a movie for this they planned extensively they arranged the gate pass got the sign from the receptionist and forged the sign of the class teacher and the principal but little did they knew on that day the principal was on the leave and for that day only the signing authority was given to the vice principal as soon as they went towards the gate and shown the gate pass they were sent back to the reception and there parents were called but that wasn't enough they were suspended too.

So always enquire before you do any sort of this.

Viva

From the very beginning of class 8 and 9, viva usually starts for everyone, which at first is considered to be nothing but as soon as you get to class 10 and class 12, you understand the real means of it and how important that it is in reality. The teachers of other schools used to come to our school for her breakfast and lunch. Their main motto was to bring out the worst answers possible from even the best students. for example, in my class 12 cbse practicals, my first practical was of economics. My roll number was 23, so the students before me had given their experiences in advance, which was like the teacher was asking from different chapters the syllabus of class 12, and someone had also given the remarks as she was asking from class 11 now I had only class 12 books I can not study and revise everything in 10 minutes, but I had a quite knowledge from 11 too so I didn't startle as others were. As soon as someone would come from giving the viva, everyone hurdled over them, and the one who was never asked in the class was the one was getting special treatment like bring chair for him drinks for him and some even saying that you are my best brother so tell me the questions asked first but as soon as he starts to speak everyone knows the answers to it so the reaction of everyone suddenly changed and the treatment that was given to him changes to nothing even the chair given to him is taken away.

Now, it was my time to go into the viva room. my brain was repeating all the interviews for the upsc exam, which I had seen yet, and according to that, I had to do everything that was required, like greeting everyone, not sitting down unless the teacher asked for it etc. So I did everything like that, but I got to know that the most important thing other than your knowledge is that you have to be more of a confident person rather than a shy person; then only you can score well.

Next comes the stream selection part after we get done with all the practicals and exams then comes the part of choosing your stream which is a very tought process I wish it was easy as soon as we got distributed with the stream selection forms it was a panic situation as if It was India vs Pakistan all were running to there groups to know what they were choosing I was clear i will take **PCMB** I wished it was easy as it sounded I thought that if it took this stream every opportunity will be open for me but when heard its real work it asks for i knew this was out of my level so got away with commerce with maths as my stream which I believe was my best decision in whole school life in academics.

Leaving all the tips behind for how to score well and stream selection, let's get onto the other chapter.

School assembly

You must have been to many assemblies held at your school, and the same was with me. Our school had 3 playgrounds at that time now it has been reduced to 1. Not only the playground but also had one auditorium which was used when someone from outside used to come for some workshop otherwise we had 2 big open type of platform with stage and all preparations being in the open and residing in India you must know how the summer can be and are yet.

The school also used to start the assembly when it was a sunny day they didn't like have mercy on the children being in the sun doesn't have many effects on the body you must be thinking but believe me sit in the sun for 2 hours with 200 people around you, you would feel like suffocating, but when those 200 are your classmates, you forget everything you must know that experience I don't have to tell you that.

But that was limited to some. I remember when I was in my seventh grade, the girl fainted in front of me. This was the first time I saw someone getting fainted in my life other than in movies; unlike in movies hitting with a punch, one gets fainted here; the punch work was done by summer.

Our school had decided that every week there has to be an assembly performed by every grade and a separate topic was allowed to every class for which they had to prepare accordingly like if the topic given was of plastic removal then we had to present a talk show speech dance and song you must be thinking how is it possible to perform a song on plastic removal well that's what I thought. Still, we should never underestimate the power of the dance teachers of our school for the praise then can even arrange the show of animals then what are we!!

Getting on with this fact for the first time, I remember the most important fight that we all used to fight was for the roles that we had to perform during the assembly, and let me tell you, it was not an easy task the roles should be suiting the image that you have built around in the school like if you got the role of showcasing the tree in the play of jungle that would be the dumbest role of the assembly that one can get no actually its second worst role the first place is awarded to the one who sings for the songs and gets even a solo performance for the same.

Let me share the real fact that happened to me. Our class was given the topic of terrorism. Being the attention-seeking topic of every time, it was our utmost duty to bring out the most factual and correct material possible being in class 8; we all took this as our responsibility, but our class teacher was very lazy about it, and why she not being organizing these types of assemblies every month she must have seen everything

Caution alert; this one was at another level.

So we got to know about the topic of assembly at the end of the day, so we thought that we would start research about it from tomorrow or if we will not be able to do it then our teacher would definitely give us the material for the same, but that's not what happened, the next day when we all met in the school the class teacher told us that she has got the message from the principal that the assembly will have to be performed after two days we all panicked and so the teacher for the first time

So that day we all decided to make arrangements that what all has to be done and how to be done but in such a chaos we gave the responsibility of an act to some stupid bunch of students of our class which I don't know how come didn't even knew the meaning of terrorism anyway i will tell you about this after a while being moving to the role I was given a role to become the narrator being active and stupendous in speaking skills it suited me, so we all decided that we will have news reporting the chief guest addressing and talk show , dance, music along with some speeches and all that took a day from two which was not our fault being just given two days for such an assembly we all had a tension that if this goes wrong this will prove to be us clowns among all the grades being frightened from this we worked as hard as we could ,like even after going out of the school our work had just started we had whatsapp groups made group calls all those who lived in same colony were made to do arrangements like posters acts and script of the speeches so that we can prepare for our assembly well.

But in the middle of this, we forgot to look after the act. We thought that the group of those Madagascar would be able to prepare for the act because we knew that we would keep the act short while the other things would be showcased for the assembly, which was not what we thought; rather, it became the opposite.

At the day of the assembly when we thought that we were very well prepared for the assembly and knew this was way before the disaster that when everything changed the play was the first one to be performed because we thought let's get end up with this so as soon as those boys entered first they put the posters out which were showing futuristic images we all thought that it must be because they will be talking about the future first then come into the past but as soon as the play started they started talking about how India will look like in future how we will rule the world and how technology will help us then there was a dance in the play itself to be performed showing the India's power but that all could not relater even the teachers were confused about it that we are talking about future or present and after that the students even left off there minds from it and let the assembly continue without the audience even the chief guest were guessing what it was about and they left off from the assembly as soon as it got out of hand the song which had to be prepared had to be have relativity about the theme which we had performed but the it was not the song was the disco song of our Bollywood movie which rather everyone enjoyed but it did not kept any relevance from the topic but that was hilarious for me as a narrator I was myself plunged that what is going on but all that mattered at the last was everyone from the students enjoyed the assembly it remembered it as a memorable one where everything was different from the theme even our class teacher was in a dilemma that what she should say to us was it good or bad after two days she came to conclusion that it was neither good nor bad but we didn't did this for some appreciation we did that because we wanted to at the last we all loved to get what we did after that hard work.

These were very awesome parts of the school, and i always enjoyed taking part in them. Even today, if anyone asks me to narrate, i always remember this incident which turned into a memorable memory.

Making more use of you

School knows the game from very much before when you took the admissions they know how to make you work for them and then also you pay them money in return after the favours and even after that you say thanks not welcome.

That's the bitter truth yes, if you have to get good marks you have work your ass off to make it happen by making the teacher believe that you are really very considerate about her or him but let's go by her, if you want to make yourself a good use pick up the notebooks from classrooms and shift them where the teacher wants might be two corridors ahead but you have to do it cause you are the one chick behind the eggs and that's not the end you have to maintain good decency during the block of that teacher like consider me I am very naughty child from the very beginning and when I am expected to be polite in the class this was a really big task especially for me but I don't blame the teacher for this as she was not the one who asked me to get good marks being marks is everything this was the whole curriculum in the whole school and not only in the school in the whole India or i should say in the most of the continents more of the preference is given to the marks nor than the skills and when we look for jobs they expect us to have good skills but how to tell them no one ever taught us that to have skills is more important than being a topper which I was but thankfully i did work on my skills side by side and didn't got much behind which is better than lacking it completely so a piece of advice from my side do not focus on just marks build skill set of your own and improve it in such a way that it makes your image unique in front of your competitors.

The school use of you does not end completely over here in the school assemblies. Being a good child image they expect you to have some responsibilities like helping all with the props and clearing them after every act but thanks to our school that this was not there at least but some of them never left a chance behind to improve and prove that they are of really help, but the main moto behind the move is just to increase the report card grade and after that class gets over with they change their attitude in front of that teacher completely consider yourself only,

Did you greet your teacher who taught you in your previous grades the time you met her before, or did you also just hide your face or start pace walking just to get rid of her? These are just basic adequate that define the personality of you as a person.

That's all that I can remember as of now in this topic, and you also remember those children in your grades who ran after the teacher to get there grades improved in their session.

School fights and funny moments

Which grade would have been faced from fights and that's natural coming from me, I was myself indulged in some of the fights and those were not simple one always it was because something of other guy being a guy who keeps control over his action and words there was hardly bad expression on teachers from me. Not that alone the headmistress mam and principal mam knew themselves about me how was my nature so whenever I got into fights, she would always ask that what happened because of which fight happened cause I had a habit to never add something into it I told truth bluntly because I knew I was not wrong in it but admitting that I could not control my temper after being done for long that was something that I had to work upon, and that's what I did in the past few years all thanks to shooting classes that I took from the seventh grade which taught me how to control myself and most importantly emotional control. But getting on with fact why I started this chapter was due to the fights and funny moments so coming back to them fights in our school were very exaggerating which had no meaning but everyone enjoyed it so did I they were mainly on the blunt topics how come you talk to any girl which was my friend how come you took my chair and many more blunt topics , the most heavy fights were of those who had a lot of back support like if they get into fight right now 20 people would be ready to come on the spot at the current moment itself so you had to choose your opponent very carefully otherwise even you escaped from the school you will get into trouble cause they would get gathered there goons in front of the school and torture you in front of everyone rather this happened only 5 to 6 times but I felt pity over them no one would come to help and this cause a big scene getting restricted from the school and what not so please avoid it whenever you can and when you get into keep it small or away from getting into the ears of school authorities at least . Let me share my experience I got into only 5 to 6 fights in my school life which took extreme points like once a student from my grade itself broke my Rakhi is just fun, but for me, that was very important being the Raksha Bandhan I was sentimentally connected to it and it was at the time of when i was in 5 grade so don't judge me for my foolishness, so what I did was I hit him with whatever I could get my hands onto, and when everyone came to stop me, he himself got every bead of it from his hands, and then only I ended up the fight after that he is still my very good friend, so I can not say the fight are always bad sometimes good friends can be made only by fights cause they are the last one to leave you during your bad time.

Coming, to the funny moments in our school I remember when I was in my pre-school time which I don't remember but my parents told me that in my class I did something exceptional which was very not expected it was the class of drawing so we were used to be provided with all the tools in the drawing which included scissors paper and all those things of no use for me being a bad artist having no hope for drawing I was playing along with the scissors and the girl in front of me was laying her hairs on my table even after a lot of warnings she again did the same thing which provoked me to do something unexpected i took the pair of scissors and cut down her pony tail my partner started laughing seeing him all class got attracted to what was happening the teacher herself curious what was so funny in drawing and when she got to know she was shocked , the girl herself was in the same shock that day I was called in the chambers of the vice principal for the first time that was indeed a funny moment for me. But that wasn't where I stopped i stomped the pencil into her hands being a nice friend of my mother her mother didn't complaint but was really annoyed so she changed her section seing my cute activities towards her **PARI**.

The prayers were the most hectic part; we were never taught the prayers separately, and being taught for the very first time, we just used to try lip sing with what was going on. Being unaware of the song we had never heard of, we would try our best to match our vibe with it same was done with the prayer in the early days; we did our best to learn it, but it was not possible, you know, learning alphabets to learning the whole new syllabus of prayers it was a big task for us small children of god. Our teacher was so bad that she started competition in this also she started this trend that those who will not open there eyes during the whole prayer will get a sticker of smile on there face and at that time smile sticker was very big thing like at that time it was equivalent to the scholars badge of today so I tried my best for getting that sticker for the starting but i couldn't succeed I used to open very small eyes towards the teacher during the prayer to see if she was watching and that particular point she would get onto my face to see if my eyes were open or closed on which I would get scared and open my whole eyes and got disqualified for the sticker so from the next day I turned over to next strategy which was not to open eyes at all which you might suppose a very easy task but ask from an early bird that how to stay in one place and we were talking about closing our eyes for about 10 minutes that's how long the prayer would be because after our prayers school song was a must which was indeed not less than an holly wood movie theme song it had such beats due to which the first day when we heard it, it was like there must be some mistake cause that's way beyond to be recognized as a prayer being so much beats but eventually we got in a habit of it due to which we would sing along with it rather more than half of the words we sang were not correct which we got to know when we were promoted to second grade . Altogether these were something which when we all friends get together laugh aloud on it and yes it is funny from our side.

The next moment to remember is during the sports block when all get too excited that they forget what is happening around them, or most importantly, they forget what is going on within them; it was the time when I was, I guess, in 5 grade, we all were going together to the sports block running on the stairs and from that I remember we all used to take up the competition that how many stairs we can jump at one time, and I used to jump of 8 to 9 stairs at a go cause I didn't have a fear of falling, which has changed with most of us as we grow up we get frightened to make decisions and think a lot of it but we should sometimes let go with the flow which is really helpful for me and proved to be beneficial i recommend you to.

Online and offline

This was the first time which was tremendously different from any other that has happened to anyone this world corona virus which affected everyone doesn't matter if it is rich poor doesn't matter if he is in develped country or under developed country it affected everyone in the world but most importantly in which we have gone to talk about his how it affected our school education which was totally different from what had be talked from the starting of the school online which was the word we have heard only in the social media WhatsApp status and that's all we have never even imagine that it would take step into a education but it is now and now also it is prevailing into our education but it is in the more positive way affecting us and then as some sort of negative way to not going to the physical classroom was one of the biggest drop back of online classes not meeting with your friends teachers smelling that lunch boxes freshness from different sort of classmates during the lunch block but actually it turn in all lunch block into every minute when we want doesn't matter where we are doesn't matter how long is it going to take to get ended up with class you can eat lunch whenever you want you can it breakfast when our you want this was one of the biggest come back of this which I enjoyed personally and so did the teachers so coming back when I was coming back from my boards of class 10 on March end of 2021 finishing boards was one of the biggest achievement of my life at that time which is mentioned for everyone when they get over with their exams but it was sports which had a different centre we had to go to the different classroom school and their different teachers so coming over with the hype of boards was itself a big achievement but I couldn't enjoy the when a single day as soon as a came back from giving my Boards I had different level of plans that I will go on a trip with my friends I will enjoy my weekend

I will play my PlayStation and finish all my games which was itself up take things for me so I had done all planning with it but that all sank into the water when I got to know that corona virus pandemic had prevailed everywhere in the world And it had entered in India too , but for me it was just normal ,in the starting I did thought that what it would be just cought cold sort of disease and many Indians did thought this way only but little did everyone knew it was the biggest curse to the world and its people it affected every economy education system in the worst way possible talking about how it affected my education and everyone out there.

Being all the plans for the after exams Seemed to be destroyed I thought that what can I do at home so I thought that maybe I could call all my friends at home for the party but cost but as soon as I got the news of locked on I was shattered that my plan of get together with my friends was also defeated. I thought that what is the point of doing all the exams when you can't even roam around free for the first in my life I had ever Heard the word lock-down even though I knew the meaning because it is just in its name that everything is going to be locked down and I thought that now I can at least enjoy with my family and that happened and I am grateful for the first month of lock down it was like everyone was enjoying it me and my father was learning to make new dishes and we started creating new recipes of an own and mom was also in a way was enjoying it even the maids in our home had gone because of the lock down but we didn't thought that it would be difficult so we distributed the task among us, was really a grateful moment for all of us to take a pause from the hectic life out there not for me because I was enjoying at the school with the friends having a party after a month of a lock down I got a note is from the school that the classes of class 12th a starting from tomorrow on a platform known as teams I was like what is it themes never heard of it and that was time when I got to know about that technology around me teams understand platform was pretty out there but I never used it because of it not user friendly base which I thought now would have changed it is still out there nevermind getting the note from the school data classes would start voice another level of excitement at least I won't be at home leaves that I thought that it won't be possible being locked down the educational institutions for themselves close down so I thought then how would I get my classes on I had to make an account on teams which was really new platform for me but I got I have it of it because if I even don't not get the habit of it I would have to take the class at least I had that level of excitement that the classes will be starting I will be atleast meeting my friends the Teachers for tenses due to this platform because due to which they were many funny activities like that teacher used to forget them Mike switch on and they would shout at they are children listening to the household overs versus it was another level of what should I say drama block for school getting all visit sometimes teachers also even for god to switch on my due to which she would under whole class and students would not even at all world because they themselves new if she got to know then she will repeat the whole letter and rather than this it was better that she did her whole lecture again and again and the last she would ask that if everyone has understood we would see from actions that she has ended the chapter and then one of the child would switch on their mic and say mam you are not audible can you please repeat what you said in the class because your mic was not on and she was like now you are telling me and it was another level of fun.

Sometimes speech about forgets that she had given control of the team's app of a class to everyone in the class, due to which some of the notorious ones would disable the mic of other children, especially the toppers that were actively participating in the class removing your enemies your friends doesn't matter, but it was another level of fun I should definitely and if you have tried it I can say that you have fully used your online classes.

Getting over with the platform where the classes were taken and how they were taken, let's begin with the exams so; the exams would definitely be another level. As you know from the term online exams, you can definitely get an idea that how the exams are going to be, we would get the notice of the exams going to be held after a week or so we would not border to open the books and let me tell you in online classes I don't know if anyone has ever seen what books for given to us by the subject teachers because we all knew that the long term was going to prevail for a long time, it was expected, and we were all in the hope that it does not even open until session ends of this class at least. In our country, the educational institutions were regularly closed down, opening for a while. The children coming back from the school were affected by the virus; the teachers were too afraid of it because of the havoc it brought to the country.

So let's become the preparation of online We would all get on the call and discuss how the preparation was going to be for this exam we all knew that the school had given the proper instruction to open the microphone and the camera all time during the exam but then also being a mind so sharp B Gordon idea that what was school do if poverty is being there or the network connection goes down and many more things that you can't even imagine of but with it I am going to discuss it here because you might use it and I know you are pretty smart yourself so you don't need my ideas so we would get onto a conference call during the exam a laptop or iPad was in front of us and our phone was just beside it the question paper when we used to see it was totally different and it was difficult I should totally agree upon it under teacher too she know that children was definitely on a cheat so at least give the questions that were not on the Google And I should say Google has benefited a lot from this there was lot of traffic on these type of sites which were never even having single viewer But for the sake of text I'm so we would see every site on the Google and a little little teacher knew that any question that you are going to put up on someone in the world might have done it and it was the case we would get every single question on the Google and so did the teacher do not get and the idea about cheating we would deliberately get two or three questions wrong so that she can at least say that you have not been cheating or you're doing it on your own and let me take my own example I did not cheat because I definitely knew that the schools were gonna open which did not in the last and I deeply regret it I did some copy I accept it but only in my 6 subject paper which got me 95 marks in class 12 boards without cheating being offline. We had make a plan that one would say to the teacher data add my network connection is going down or can I go to the washroom and then we all would one by one closer camera and turn off the microphone get on the conference call and discuss all the questions at that time discord was also one of the platform for cheating which I had heard from my friend that you can come up on it and we will discuss the answer but I knew that I had prepared well for that exam even though I had prepared for every exam more than my capacity but the exam was totally different from what we were taught in the classthe questions which were I was not able to get for the one I used to search on Google and get an answer for it and so did I send it to my friends because they used to call me again and again if I do not answer the call they would text me ping me and that was really annoying for me during the exam because even though it was online exam there was a fixed time limit you had to submit your exam within one hour one hour 10 minutes and if you get even a single minute up from it the exam was not gonna get uploaded this was something that created trouble for us because some questions took more than 10 minutes 20 minutes time for at least getting jotted down or taking time from Google was an extra effort.

It was not just the teachers that used to forget their mikes were on, but many of us, let me take an example, actually a real-life example. I should say my friend texted me that he woke me up at a time of attendance, and he was snoring. I don't know How come his mic got unmuted and his snoring sounds were taking over the teacher's voice, so she called his name two to three times and even called his phone but it was all useless after giving the call to his mother he said present mam I was in the washroom so couldn't hear you and everyone was laughing in the class the teacher said that you might also be sleeping in the washroom then. The online classes had their own fun.

The assemblies had adjusted to being online, and you can imagine if offline was so much fun, then what would happen online? Our class had the first PPT in the presentation for the assembly. We had started preparation a week before the PPT had an awesome scope, and it was beautifully presented, but it could not happen in front of the vice principal and principal mam. As soon as the assembly had started, we started with the prayer to thank almighty

After that we started with the PPT the one who was given With incharge to present it was not present in the meeting the class teacher was constantly calling the name again and again after a while I check the list and told to class in charge that not only she was calling the wrong guy but wrong I was also not present in the class after that I didn't knew that this would get a catch hold of vice principle she asked in very anger tone from the teacher if she had not practiced it with the students Now technical glitches are although have become a part of a life but we now also cannot accept them and specially at the time of such type of event where the heads are present our class teacher had humbly requested principle to wait for a while she called the student number and got to know that her laptop was corrupted Now that was very lame excuse we easily new that she must have not woken up yet and that would happen she texted one of us and while all of our phones were with the teacher because those who were able to come to the school were allowed and me and group of friends were there no when the phone Bing the teachers saw the message was from the one who was in charge of the ppt she sent what should I do now I have just woken up and starting the laptop The teacher had ignored this fact and let the assembly begin because it was getting late . Also, she had the power of marks, so she could very well whenever take revenge, but she was very nice, so she forgave her. After the assembly, we all took a breath of relief.

This was a new experience for everyone, and somewhat that which will never be forgotten even will be passed on to the next generation.

Trips

One of the most important and awesome parts of the school is trips that too outstation, especially you will get to know why.

The trips in our school were mainly organised by the third party and not by the school itself, and due to that sole reason the marketing strategy has to be good by there side then only many students would decide to join the trip

But as you know, they just waste their cost for this if i would have been given the marketing head i would have saved them hell lot of money and saved there time also because they might not know that when you organize a trip you just need some students to confirm there trip then the others will join the chain and see there friends going so, they will also go and join. The trips that our school mostly organized were international and hardly any domestic or one-day trips, but all of them took their enjoyment to the next level as the school friends are the ones with which you have the best days of your life if i talk about school or then of trips, trips are more awesome because you get to see and enjoy whole day with your friends.

Let me first take the example of the trip that were organized by the school and was more like a camp, what they used to write in the circular of the trip entrance.

The first trip that I got into was school camp which was an adventure camp, and you can see the name suggests you get excited. Then just imagine how I would have reacted to being a child and seeing myself enjoying it. Now before any this sort of trip, the school had the basic motive to know why it was important for the students, so they used to make workshop arrangements. They were not well informed to the teachers themselves, so the best part of them was when it was maths block or any other subject block it used to be because we would get a sign of relief from them anyways let's get back to the workshop it was usually arranged in the multipurpose room of our school I didn't know that the name given to it was to be taken seriously because doesn't matter what it be workshop, mun trial, competition, celebrations of some events, dance training, music class, everything that you can imagine, so it was multipurpose in short.

So, the whole grade used to be called at one time, and you can imagine how the voice would be while walking of everyone at the same time. Let me tell you, and it was horrendous. It used to be at that peak that I was not able to hear what the other student was saying unless spoken loudly. That's also the reason why some students who do not use to speak loudly start shouting suddenly because it has become our daily habit, anyways coming back to the trips going by the one I took the adventure camp. So, when we reached out to the multipurpose hall, it took the teachers around 20 minutes just to settle us, and when the voices got downed a little, but only then did the vice principal and Principle these type of events or any other events in our school were always having the guests as them only hardly any new one, or if some teacher is on the edge to get the promotion, she also gets a seat beside them. So continuing further reaching to the multipurpose hall was not easy, but we did it. Now the teacher would take the opportunity to make a speech on some facts about why this meeting has been organized but who doesn't know about it the grades that you called before already had told and we all Knew what was gonna happen further. Carrying With the act Like we are the 1st one to the audience. After the boring speech, there would generally be a song that would have come up instantly by the teachers of the singing Academy. Then everyone's eyes would light up as soon as the projector would start Because we knew there were animation or videos would have been coming which would cover us, but that was generally an assumption that would never come true, And we are still also waiting for that assumption to happen But as soon as the trip images that would be happening in the trip would come we all used to get excited Seeing all the monuments we would visit seeing all the food that we're gonna enjoy during the trip most important enjoying with all the buddies that we want to spend time As soon as this starts Everyone around would talk to their friends that if they're willing to go over there because then only they would plan for it. There would be a whole presentation arranged for it As soon as last slide would be projected We all would be at the extent of finishing the pie we would be At the top level of excitement And then we used to think that the form would be given to us right now but it never came true they used to say that the teachers would would provide the form for this And you can get a sign from the parents Now the most important thing after this was how how to get parents ready for it because it used to be written on the phone at last paragraph Anything that happens to the student better be Anything then the school won't be responsible now seeing the Dodge line we used to think that what would be what would happen to us But anyway that form was given to us after 2 to 3 days and never at the time of the presentation But as soon we reached homes we used to talk With the parents to make them familiarize About this activity which was gonna happen in the school and for that Particular week be used to get indulged in many of the academic activities Giving our best and the revision test providing each and every unit test our full efforts. Just for the sake of yes on the form and the sign of the parents we used to do all our chores at the house Now after all the efforts that we have done for the signature we would submit that form to the teacher and wait eagerly for that Camp to start I'm finally skipping to the day when the Camp would have to be started We would wake up before the sunshine's and get ready with a bright and dream and eagerly waiting for all the activities and A-day waiting ahead of us Which has to be filled with joy achievement and fun activities So skipping to the day when we reached the school We were filled with joy seeing all our classmates moving up to the classrooms And with an awesome and a different level of zeal in them even I was included in them After the regular marking of the students for who came or not after that we all used to run towards the ground area where our instructor was waiting we were divided into different sort of groups like scorpions zebras and many different names that were given to us but the most important thing was that we were having an another level of excitement to do the activities which we had never done never done with the friends. You know the activities that we have done before, but with the friends, they seem to be like new the experience the talks and what all we cannot do with

the friends have a different charm, you know After divided into groups, we were put into the 1st activity, which was group picture and I have been waiting to get it until today, and it has been almost five years, and still, there is no tracking of it I just can't believe that is possible, but you know everything can be possible by the school.

Anyway, moving on to the next, we all used to get the number pani which you won't believe was too good. I don't know how I remember it now. Also that I took almost five glasses of it. So it was the time of the first activity, which was the zip line. The most exciting activity was set up from the top floor of the school, which was five floors from the ground and to the ground it must be around 500 meters and when the instructor put you towards the ledge that's the most dangerous part for most of the students and the instructor doesn't force everyone to do it but said this to everyone that "the real ride starts after this," and it was actually what he said the adventure truly starts after this the most dangerous activity ones done make the experience of other ones more interesting and more enjoyable. Many of the children used to start crying, and most of them were girls; they used to make their own group that should we do this one or not or rather just do another one, and like this, their whole adventure camp gets converted into a gossip camp which lasts ever ending.

The activities were of very good level and adventurous like military net, zip zap, between the bridge many more but during the activities, there is some other level of tension going on behind the head on many of us which performance pressure like what will they think if I fell in this activity so many activities are just avoided to make an excuse from the laugh, but that's actually a good part of it, it unveils the harsh reality that people will laugh at you if you make any mistake but why am I telling you guys you must have seen it in many motivational quotes at your Instagram feed.

Anyways, trips like these are very interesting. I should rather use an adventure camp other than trips cause the real trip adventure is gonna begin now,

My first trip that i had ever gone with the school to the outstation was Nainital which is quite popular place for trip among Indians and i had visited there with my family for about 3 times already I ain't gonna repeat myself with the workshop and all that stuff that I have discussed how school make us mad to go over these trips but yes for the first time outstation that was pretty new to all of us like is that really happening we couldn't believe our eyes that school was taking us to the outstation being listening and getting excited is one part but making parents ready to send us outstation without them and trusting school was a big task and it was sure that it was not going to be easy and it became true in no time for me as soon as I reached home I showed the form of trip to mom and she said the answer for it very simply no , even when i insisted after a lot of efforts she said talk to your father and if he says yes i will also agree little did mom knew i had a promise kept from father which i was looking to make use of and after that also it became a lot difficult because being a 10 11 year old child it was very difficult to convince

parents that it will be beneficial for us now i even said it was going to be a knowledgeable trip and hearing all that sort of things which made the trip look so good it became more difficult after it was decided that it will happen only when i score 95 percent above in maths unit test so I got taking all my spirits and motivating me for getting full but as soon as two chapters were done I thought that I have got myself into trouble and even if I study for 24 hours a day maths will never get finished and even if finished I won't know what to do in the questions in the paper because you yourself, must have experienced that what taught to us in the school classroom doesn't tally even a little bit what is asked from us in the question paper and that's really annoying but luckily I didn't study from the prescribed book of the school I got to the stationary and told him give me the best book for the exam I gave my full energy in memorizing all the questions which got to be the same as in the question paper of the test which got me 96 percent, after this I though now there will be no stopping from getting my parents get the form filled little did I knew the last date of the form had already been past and because i took leaves from the school during the exam I had no idea of it now after humongous request from the teacher and telling the story behind it she talked to the trip in charge and said to arrange one more seat for the trip and that moment gave me hell of a joy it was like when I lost all my hope I got the hand of the god.

So coming back to home I told my parents a week past the trip itself I was given instructions by the parents that how to stay properly like drinking mild everyday doesn't matter if you have to order from the hotel but drink it many more like don't leave the group at any time don't eat anything from the stranger and so on cause if I discuss this it is never ending cause parents are the one who cares about there child moving back to the trip planning our school had arranged two to three workshops about rules to be followed during the trip like never leaving the teacher when outside don't buy anything without informing the teacher and many more so during that workshop I remember I had a pouch which was having the most expensive pen collection that I had made which included all top notch pens cause at that time this was flex among us not the I phones , I don't know who did it but my pouch with my whole collection got stolen from my bag itself it was like what should I do I was deeply regretting why i had gone to the workshop even got scolded and that was obvious loosing 5 to 10 grand worth of pens was a great loss for me. I got over with it just by keeping my mind set like that. It was just something i had to sacrifice for the trip, and eventually, in two days, I got over with it, although I am on the look for that guy.

Anyways the day came when i had to go. I was really very excited, and for that reason I couldn't sleep even for a moment. I was thinking of the plans I needed to do, what to eat, what to buy, and a lot of those ideas had taken over the sleep which happens with me today also when I have to go on the trips I have so many plans going on that I am unable to sleep. So, after waking up from fake sleep, I got up with real enthusiasm for the trip to commence. My mom cried when i was leaving. My father said to take care of yourself and enjoy the trip as much as you can. After that, I reached the school, and we were not given any instructions that if phones were allowed or not, which was a very debated topic. being alone for the first time, we had the excitement that we would have phones in our hands every time, but as soon as I reached the reporting classroom, we all were showing off the phones that we had brought for the trip, but that caught the attention of the trip in charge she immediately said everyone to deposit there phones in the school itself, and when we will come back all would get them back, so our photos plan was coming to an end, but we got an assured from the class teacher which was accompanying on the trip that she would click the photos and provide the phone calls too for talking to parents. that's when we got some satisfaction, after that we got call from our in charge to assemble to board on the bus we were on the next level of excitement as I am writing about it i am getting energized too, anyways getting back I rushed towards corner seat as I love to sit on them to enjoy the view. as soon as the bus started, its ac turned its vent towards me, I rotated it, and i don't know how come it broke the teacher when i saw it I thought I would scream but being sweet, she just told me to give it to the conductor after that our group had pre-planned that what all foods we will bring along, so we took out and started our trip having almost 30 chips with 20 to 25 biscuits and what not chocolates, gum, etc. We were having an another level of fun. After two hours, i suppose the bus came to a halt for food and the washroom. We were enjoying ourselves in the washroom, also banging the doors with putting water on each other it was like we became kids again; wait .. We were kids!! but we were enjoying ourselves like newbies. The food was not good being at the dhaba, we can not expect much but being with all the best ones everything turns into a moment.

Then we boarded the bus again and then when the teacher took a number of the student she came to know that two were missing we all were shocked they were neither with us at the eating place after wasting half hour we got to know that they were locked inside the washroom of dhaba and were crying out loud at least the teacher found them, so we were full now from the stomach and in the bus too.

Coming back to the bus, we all were really enjoying it to the fullest, singing songs and playing Ludo, in which full-on cheating was going on, which was not intentional but due to the driving way, but we were taking full opportunity to get to the house. After sitting on the bus for 8 hours, we were finally at our destination; it was not like I had never visited Jim Corbett national park, but it was the first time with friends, so it had its own fun. We were allotted the rooms in pair of 4 now after entering in the room the matter of the discussion among us was that there was one bed one couch and one extra bed who is gonna sleep were being a trip of 3 nights four days it was a tough decision I was already in the bed so I didn't have to worry about Anything and for others, I gave the idea of playing rock paper scissors so at least one can get a fair chance. After a day's rest, we were taken on a safari in the jungle. It was really nice, but at the same time, my clothes were all covered in dust which made me take a bath again. Anyways we all were not surprised to see animals, but it was the opposite seeing such different beings hooting and shouting. Seeing even small creatures, the animals must be shocked. After that, we had a full stomach dinner and called our parents on the teacher's phone. Told them we were fine in an enthusiastic way, so they were also relieved that our children were safe and enjoying themselves. Not soon after we were into the dj night where we were dancing like animals jumping over each other like it's the first time we were listening the song but that was awesome I never danced like that, then it was time to go to the bed now it is not easy to got to the bed is it specially it was were less time so to enjoy we had to arrange something, we all four mates arranged the game of ringing bells of hotel rooms and running the one caught will not be allowed into the bed or couch he will have to sleep on the floor so seeing the game it was more like excitement rather than having fear of the punishment we all got down to the lobby where we all rang the bell at the same time of the teachers itself we didn't knew it was there room otherwise we would have brought others too, to take advantage for at least ones in there life of the teachers they came out and we were shouting by taking random names of the students as if they were the one who were ringing the bell it was really awesome but I don't know how come one teacher found out that we were the one who were ringing the bell so he came to our room ringing the bell we were ready for something like this so we faked as if we were in deep sleep but we forgot the we didn't switched off the lights of the room so the teacher questioned it and naturally the answer that would come into our mind was that he went to the washroom so switched on the light so he got assured that we were not the one and left. From this, I would also like to bring the fact of those who are hypocrites like being nice from the front and on one side giving negative info to the teachers, and if you are one of them, please don't do it spoils the fun, and if you don't know what is so good in it try it yourself anyways, getting back to the breakfast call at the morning which woke us up, we were fighting who was going to bath first so again did the same rock paper scissors game in which I won so I had a good time. This time we went shopping after that and the teacher accompanying us clearly gave us instructions don't buy Anything without prior letting the teacher know as if we were very naive and I got my eyes on the new lighter which I thought was very nice I never used one in real life so having an emblem of Micheal Jackson it attracted me it was roller lighter which I today also remember was sold to me at a very high rate as I was a child and I make it wrapped very nicely such that no one can know if it was a lighter or a book wrapped. So long story short, I was successful in getting it safely to my father as a gift showpiece. It was a very nice trip, but on our way to the market, there were hills on which the bus was traveling so the bus got engine problem in the middle of the hill, so we all were scared as the bus was going back again and again and on our back, it was just a never-ending valley as soon as I was seeing it I was getting frightened, but we all were taken out of the bus, and after waiting for an hour a new bus managed to take us to the market.

It was an unforgettable trip that gave me a lot of memories and a new way to enjoy the trip.

Never ever miss a chance to go on a trip with friends.

Farewell

Farewell, which has everything to do with even if We are in our primary grades, we are always excited for it doesn't matter if it will be given to us after five years or more, but we await for that day extensively, and same was with me.

In my early grades, I used to see students dressed as gentlemen and ladies, which used to excite me because of how good they looked and not only how the school used to organize everything. It was a great feeling seeing the whole auditorium getting new decorations, planning new games and new activities, making juniors dance to vulgar songs, And whatnot.

The most interesting activity was deciding who would be head boy and girl, which was a very rigorous process in our school, being five students from every class and seven sections that used to be tough for the teachers too.

Not only that, academic achievers were so given awards, and a separate ceremony was organized for them

Let's begin with this ceremony itself. It was known as an investiture ceremony where all the awards were presented to the academic holders or to those who have performed in any activity to showcase their achievements.

I have been getting one hundred percent attendance for the past ten years, and not only that, in class 10, I was presented as an academic holder and the same in class 12 too. Not showing off but gave this highlight to showcase the discrimination done by the school when I used to get the 100 percent attendance award or anyone who got it was placed at the last of the ceremony, which I believe is the worst appreciation to be given that child has not taken single leave in the whole year and left all his programs aside for this award which at last proves to be nothing but I used to do it for the different purpose I was into shooting sport as you know and which motivated me to come every day, I thought if I am coming for shooting then what is the harm in attending school so if any teacher is reading this kindly make that award more attractive so that it is at least equal to what the student has sacrificed to come to that boring lectures.

Moving on with the flow, even though we are very excited to attend farewell, it does ignore the fact that it will be the last time when all your school friends sit together and talk; this was not in my mind when I craved to attend it during my early grades, and now it was too late to go back to live the memories again. Even though most of us are in touch through social media, a like-on image can not take the place of real talk. All those awesome friends get contracted and get on to 2 or 3 if lucky even 5 but all those promises come to an end and just so the all the best thing turns to memories. But that's the phase of life now. no one would wish to go to school every of their life and nothing after death, just a name on the tombstone with a title as passed class 12 with distinction but pursuing my school path with dreams that just got to an end.

Just like when we all used to get results of boards running towards the school with new joy and sweet boxes to celebrate with the teachers as they taught us well, i remember as soon as I got my result of class 12 with a percentile of 94.8 percent i was whooped over with joy and was just waiting to get to the school. as soon as i reached the school got to know that the session for the new students was already started and was not able to meet all the teachers, but after a wait of 2 hours at the reception I was already annoyed, which caused me to meet just a few of the teachers as all others were teaching all of them were very proud and joyed of my performance. I even met all my primary grade teachers and was known by almost all of them. Even the teachers whom i had never heard the name of knew who I was cause of the grace of other teachers. It was not like I was the topper; there were 10 or more students who got more than this, but I was happy as something is better than nothing.

Even the feeling of boards is still also with me. i remember how i hurried myself to get to the centre before time my paper was to be started at 10 and i kept myself ready to be there by sharp 9, as soon as the car was moving towards the examination centre my heart was pounding up and down, but mom and dad along with my sister were all along with me, so it was just for a while. After reaching and settling down at the centre, seeing two boards in charge in the same class was just very frightening. But sitting with all the class friends was something that made me go over that feeling. As soon as the paper ended, I used to just go towards my outside without talking about the paper cause that caused tension along with trouble of if I did it right or wrong. Anyways it was very different giving papers in different schools with different teachers which we have never seen some very tough with some along butter.

Anyway, coming back from the tombstone as soon as the board paper are going to get started just a month before the school decides to host a farewell which is not alone before boards there was a pooja organized by the school in which our school teacher of sanskrit language was himself the pandit{priest} of that Pooja we were like how deep can school go to save money. but we also didn't know that Pooja he did was absolutely according to the procedure and someone made a rumour that he has his own Pooja agency and he goes to different homes to do Pooja for a side income that news got to become a disaster for him because the news quickly got spread across the teachers which included vice principle and principle mam. We all got to know he was called into the office of her but don't know after that he might be yet in search of that guy.

Coming back to the school auditorium, the farewell was very well organized, and we all got an invite to be there with the theme of formals which is common in all the schools, and I was amazed to see how all those who wore clothes as no one would ever wear were wearing top-notch clothes girls were dressed like they got the parlour on them I am not saying that they were not good, but they were extremely good that's all I am saying.

Let me start from the beginning. first there was a rally organized by boys in which all of the cars were a top-notch from Audi r8 to Bentley along with the bikes ranging from Ducati all were moving in one direction with parking lights on where ever we all were moving people were recoding all of our activity it was actually the best feeling of farewell which was not given by school. after that we all reached school in which our juniors did the worst dance possible to entertain us taking photos with teachers and all our friends with giving interview for mister me for the school.

It was very something that can't be expressed after that we went to our after party which was a hell of a party. Awesome drinks, dance, and just like in movies, we do know what we are doing; that was the feeling. coming back from that was like the day came to an end. i was pretty heavy that this was the last one with all of us together, but it was to a new beginning.

About the author

Mridul Nanda an eighteen year old teen who has decided to get experience of everything, having tried almost every sports having passion of writing songs , playing music instruments , creating a start-up and now a BOOK. Being an optimistic guy always looking for opportunities and with a vision of fulfilling all dreams.

Having experience in the field of shooting 10 meter air rifle for almost 7 years having national renowed shooter certificate.

9 789357 043076

Printed by Libri Plureos GmbH in Hamburg, Germany